BINKLEY'S BOTTLENECK

Binkley's Bottleneck

WRITTEN AND ILLUSTRATED BY
Stella F. Rapaport

G. P. Putnam's Sons   New York

Other books by the same author

A WHITTLE TOO MUCH

REINDEER RESCUE

© 1956 BY STELLA F. RAPAPORT

Published on the same day in the Dominion of
Canada by Thomas Allen, Ltd., Toronto

Library of Congress Catalog Card Number: 56-10270

MANUFACTURED IN THE UNITED STATES OF AMERICA

Many thanks to my son, Myron, for his assistance in technical know-how.

ANDY watched the signal across the river. The man pulled the rope, the wooden arm jerked up and a bell jangled at the end of it. It meant a car was waiting for the ferry to take it across.

"Someone's 'cross the river, Gramp!" called Andy.

Grandpa Binkley didn't answer. He was busy chatting about his ferry to the passengers. For over fifty years he had been running Binkley's Faithful Ferry back and forth, back and forth, from shore to shore, across the broad Massapee River.

7

"And everybody knows that from early spring till the last frost freezes the river solid, they can cross this river on Binkley's Faithful Ferry," said Grandpa proudly.

"Yes, indeed," agreed a passenger. "Only trouble is," he chuckled, "we sometimes have a very long, long wait to get *on* the ferry! Look now."

The ferry was approaching Binkley's Landing in Springvale. A long line of cars was waiting, bumper to bumper. It was true, the little ferry would not be able to take them all in one trip. Binkley's Faithful Ferry carried, at most, six to eight cars. It was just a homemade wooden barge powered by a small boat attached to one side. An underwater cable, tied to each shore, guided it across against the pull of the swift current.

"I'll be able to take care of everybody," said Grandpa Binkley, "just as soon as I get my new ferry. It will be a modern streamlined beauty — a Diesel electric — able to go in either direction without turning around, and no cable underneath." His eyes shone at the thought of it.

"It will carry fifty cars at one time!" Andy chimed in.

"But even a larger, up-to-date ferry won't be able to handle all the traffic," said the passenger. "There's no other way to cross the Massapee River for seventy miles up and down. What we need is a bridge. I hear the State is working on it now."

"Fiddlesticks!" snorted Grandpa. "I've been hearing that for more than ten years. It's talk — just talk."

Andy wondered why Grandpa always got cross when anyone spoke of a new bridge across the Massapee. He glanced again at the signal across the river. There were six or seven cars now. What with all those waiting on this side in Springvale, it looked like Binkley's Faithful Ferry was in for a heavy traffic jam. Soon all the cars would begin to toot their horns.

"Grandpa!" he shouted. "Excuse me, Gramp."

Grandpa Binkley turned to him. Andy shook his hand pointing across the river.

"Oh — oh, everyone is in a hurry nowadays." Grandpa hustled the people back into their cars. "Have a good trip!"

The drivers started their motors and the cars rolled off the ferry. They rumbled up the wooden ramp of the dock of Binkley's Landing, up the road and away. Eight cars and three bicycles rolled down the ramp onto the ferry. Those who couldn't get on fretted and complained.

"Something's gotta be done about this. We haven't got all day!"

"What a bottleneck!"

"We'll be back as soon as we can!" shouted

Grandpa Binkley cheerfully. "Hurry, Andy, show the cars where to go. Tell the drivers to be sure their motors are turned off and the brakes are on and slip the chocks under the front wheels."

Andy was already doing that. He guided the cars on the ferry — one to the left, one to the right, in two rows with the bicycles in between, to keep the barge balanced. Then he untied the hawser from the bit on the dock and tossed the rope aboard the ferry. He raised the ramp and closed it, drew the heavy chain across, and raised his hand to Grandpa.

"All aboard! Ready to go!"

In the tiny cabin, Grandpa pulled the cord of the ship's bell. It clanged a warning to other boats to steer clear. He pushed the lever of the idling motor to Go. The ferry slipped away from the dock and chugged across the river.

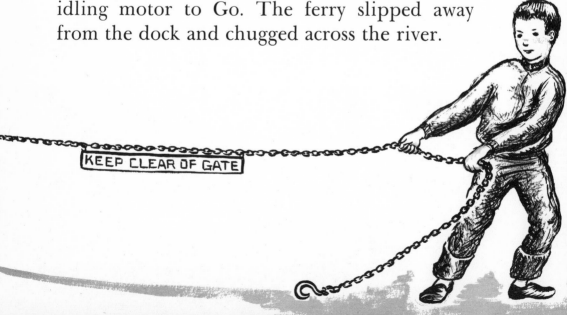

KEEP CLEAR OF GATE

When Grandpa took over the motor, Andy collected the fares. Sometimes Andy ran the motor while Grandpa took the fares. Strangers exclaimed over the "quaint" little ferry, and Andy, like his Grandpa, enjoyed telling about the first Binkley's Faithful Ferry of fifty years ago. It was a steam ferry pulling on a heavy chain across the river from Springvale to Appleby Hills. It carried everything from horses and wagons, carriages and bicycles, to cows or a flock of sheep on their way to market. Springvale was a busy river port then, with all kinds of sail-boats and steamboats putting in at her docks

from up and down the Massapee River.

"Sooner or later, those old steam ferries would catch on fire and burn down," said Andy. "After several years, Grandpa built a new ferry with a Model T Ford car motor which turned paddlewheels on the side."

"Yep, Binkley always keeps up with progress!" Grandpa thrust his head out of the cabin window. "Each Binkley's Faithful Ferry I built was bigger and better than the one before. Even this tug has had its day. It's been in service a long time. Wait till you see my next ferry!"

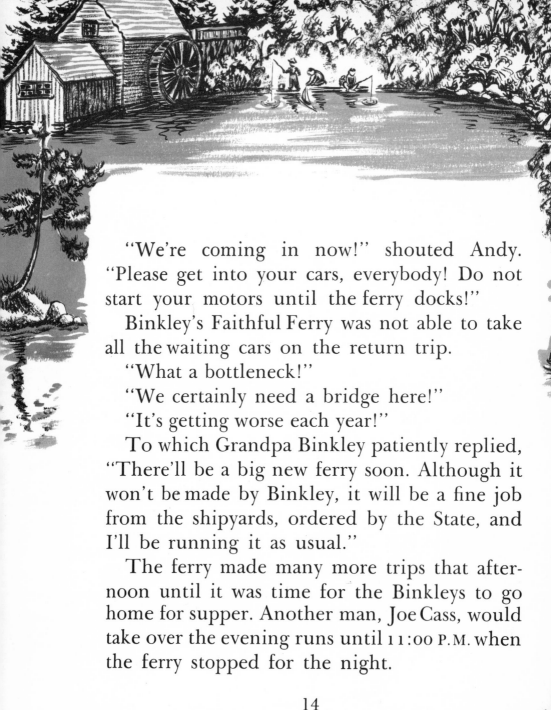

"We're coming in now!" shouted Andy.
"Please get into your cars, everybody! Do not
start your motors until the ferry docks!"

Binkley's Faithful Ferry was not able to take
all the waiting cars on the return trip.

"What a bottleneck!"

"We certainly need a bridge here!"

"It's getting worse each year!"

To which Grandpa Binkley patiently replied,
"There'll be a big new ferry soon. Although it
won't be made by Binkley, it will be a fine job
from the shipyards, ordered by the State, and
I'll be running it as usual."

The ferry made many more trips that afternoon until it was time for the Binkleys to go
home for supper. Another man, Joe Cass, would
take over the evening runs until 11:00 P.M. when
the ferry stopped for the night.

14

On one side of Binkley's Landing in Spring-vale, an old water wheel stood idle. Small boys fished in the quiet cove around it. On the other side of the ferry slip, Andy's father ran a busy boat yard. His older brother, Paul, was pulling

on a long line of rowboats, each tied to the other.

"It's time to go home for supper!" shouted Andy.

"Okay," replied Paul. "Give me a hand with these boats!"

"Go ahead," said Grandpa. "Joe Cass will be here soon and I'll join you."

Andy ran over. He nimbly hopped from one rowboat to the other and tied the last one to an iron ring at the end of the pier. He helped Paul secure the moorings of the larger boats. They carried the oars and outboards and safety cushions into the boathouse. Father Binkley clamped the outboard motors to the racks and laid away the fishing lines, rods and tackle.

Andy's sister, Ellie, gave the counter in the refreshment stand a last wipe. "I'm ready, too. Whew! What a busy afternoon — everyone was thirsty!"

By the time they were all seated in the car, Grandpa was with them too. It was a short ride through the village of Springvale to their home on the other side. At the supper table, the children talked about school and what happened down at the river after school where they all helped Dad and Grandpa. Mother gossiped about this and that she heard down in the village.

Then Paul said, "You know that new highway they're building up over the hill? And everybody is guessing where it's going to? Well, it's leading right to a brand new bridge that is going to be built across the Massapee River!"

"Gee! It will be wonderful to have a bridge over the river!" exclaimed Andy.

Grandpa Binkley banged his fist down on the table. "Why do you all listen to such gossip? Somebody starts a rumor and it spreads and spreads till nobody knows what he's talking about."

The family stared at Grandpa in amazement. It was so seldom he lost his temper.

"There's no need to get angry," soothed Mother, "after all, the State has been buying up people's property along the route of the new road and everyone knows that sooner or later

a bridge will *have* to be built to take care of all the traffic."

"What's my ferry for?" snapped Grandpa.

"Well, Dad," said Father Binkley, "it really can't handle all of the people and cars that pass this way. It's too slow for modern traveling. Many cars go fifty miles or more out of their way so as not to be held up at the ferry."

"Hurry, hurry, hurry," mocked Grandpa, "the whole world is in a hurry — and don't know where they're going!" He stalked out of the room in a huff.

Nothing more was said. Quietly, the boys went upstairs to do their homework, while Ellie helped Mother clear the table and do the dishes. Father Binkley read his newspaper. Andy was puzzled. He went over to his father. "Dad, why was Grandpa so angry?"

"If a new bridge is built, Andy, Binkley's Faithful Ferry will stop running."

Andy was stunned. "What do you mean?"

Father Binkley spoke softly. "There won't be any use for it; people will all use the new roads and new bridge."

"But Grandpa is going to get a new big electric ferry!"

Father shook his head. "No ferry can take the place of a good bridge over the river — with no waiting, no stopping summer or winter. The bridge and new roads will build up this part of the country."

So that was why Grandpa was so upset whenever anyone spoke of a new bridge — he *knew* the bridge would replace his ferry! It had always seemed to Andy that Binkley's Faithful Ferry would go on forever — a newer, more modern ferry, of course, but still Binkley's Ferry faithfully running between Springvale and Appleby Hills. What would Grandpa do without his ferry?

Andy made up his mind to find out for himself whether a bridge was really being started or whether it was just idle talk. The next day, right after school, he ran down to Binkley's Landing, drank a glass of milk and stuffed his mouth with cookies.

"Dad, may I use one of the boats?"

"Aren't you helping Grandpa with the ferry today?" asked Father Binkley.

"Yes, later on. I just want to go somewhere first."

"Help yourself." His father asked no further questions. Perhaps he guessed where Andy was going.

Andy carried a small five-horsepower outboard motor down to one of the boats and clamped it on. He checked the gas and oil and filled the spare tank. He pulled the starter cord — once, twice, three times — and the motor caught on and chugged. He eased the boat away from the pier, in and out among the moored boats and out midstream. He waved to Grandpa on the ferry as he passed by.

"I'll be back later to help, Gramp!"

Grandpa waved back. There were only a few cars on the ferry. Things were slow that after-

noon and he would be be able to manage alone.

Andy opened up at full throttle. Urged on by a fast current, the boat sped swifty down the river trailing a long feather of white foam. Andy looked back at Grandpa's little ferry. Back and forth, back and forth, it curved from Binkley's Landing in Springvale to the gently sloping farmland of Appleby Hills, on the opposite shore. The village hall tower rose up tall above the thick green trees. Here and there a slanting roof caught a shaft of sunlight and twinkled back. Little white houses peeked out through the woods. Across, in Appleby Hills, the fields were green and gold and yellow, the orchards a mass of soft pink and white bloom.

In a short while, Andy turned around the bend of the Massapee River, cut his motor and drifted. This was where Paul said the bridge would be built. There was no sign of any con-struction — the forest looked untouched on both sides of the river. A kingfisher swooped down and deftly plucked a flapping fish out of the water. A muskrat stole among the rushes at the river's edge and slid into a hole in the bank. Grandpa was right. It was all just gossip.

Rat-tat-tat—what was that? Some kind of machinery was at work!

"Hello there!" a man's voice called out.

Andy searched in the direction the voice came from. A man stood near the water. Andy had not noticed him before. He must have just come out of the woods. Andy pulled his boat in toward shore.

"I'm an engineer working on the new bridge. Could you give me a lift across the river, son?"

For a moment, Andy didn't answer. Finally, he said, "You could use the ferry down at Binkley's Landing."

The man laughed. "Oh, Binkley's Bottleneck? I don't have that much time. I have to get to the other side of this river — today."

Andy reddened. He didn't like anyone to laugh at Grandpa's ferry. "You'll have to swim across. I'm busy." He turned angrily away and pulled the cord of his motor.

"Wait, son, I didn't mean any harm. It's a fine ferry. Let me explain. Work is being started on the new bridge — on this side and across the river too. Our boat carrying workers just left. I must get across very quickly and you came by at just the right time. Here's a dollar for your trouble."

Andy glanced at the money but didn't take it. He was more interested in the bridge. Here was clearly the man who could tell him more.

"All right, I'll take you across. I don't see any work going on," Andy added.

"When we get to the other side, come with me, I'll show you."

The man got into the boat. He said his name was Duffy. Andy felt cross at himself for going with this man who had insulted Grandpa's ferry, but he just had to find out more.

When they reached the opposite shore, Andy tied his boat to a willow and followed Duffy. Some few hundred yards ahead he saw a large clearing that had been hidden by the thick growth of trees along the river bank. Heavy bulldozers were mowing down the trees like a plow going through a cornfield. The thick blades

25

scraped the stones and bushes right off and out of the ground. Another machine was scooping the earth out of a hill and moving it further on to fill in a hollow.

"What are they drilling over there?" Andy pointed to a rocky place.

"They're boring holes for sticks of dynamite which will break up the solid rock," said Duffy. "Look over to the left, Andy — those men are digging a trench for drainage pipes."

"So many kinds of work go on at the same time!" exclaimed Andy.

"Sure do!" Duffy nodded. "Yet each job dovetails with the others. First the ground must be cleared and leveled. Hills are sliced down, hollows are filled, and rocks in the way are blasted and removed."

They walked over to a shack nearby which served as headquarters. A foreman came out with a roll of papers under his arm. "Here are the blueprints," he said, spreading out the papers, "with every detail of the highway. Your hometown won't be left out — although it's off the main highway, a spur will be built right into Springvale."

"How do you know where to build?" asked Andy. In spite of himself, he was interested.

Duffy smiled. "Years of planning have already gone into this highway and bridge."

"I know there's been a lot of talk about it."

"More than just talk, Andy. The country was mapped out by surveyors — exactly, even to the inch. Every hill, every dip in the ground, every brook and river was marked and measured. The path the new highway would take was drawn. Then the property along the right of way was bought by the State from those who owned it. For the bridge, the Massapee River had to be studied very carefully; not only the shores of the river on both sides, but the currents and, of course, the river bed. A bridge has to rest on a foundation and the men had to find out what was in the river bottom and how deep they

would have to dig to come to hard rock or firm ground. Even the weather in this part of the country was studied. How fast do the winds blow? How hot and how cold does it get? How thick is the ice on the river in winter? Then the bridge engineers decided on the kind of bridge best suited to this particular river, this country, and the traffic conditions here."

"What kind are they going to build?" asked Andy.

"A suspension bridge. That is a bridge that is suspended or hung from two main towers. The towers rest on a foundation built on the river bottom. Think of a bridge, Andy, as a continuation of the road. The traffic must run over it smoothly and swiftly. But you see, there's a crossroads here — the river. It too carries traffic — the ships and boats. They have to be able to move on the river without bumping into the highway or bridge. So the bridge over this river will be built high enough to permit even the tallest ships to pass underneath. Sometimes, when it is not practical to build a high enough bridge, they build a bridge that opens up to let the boats go through."

"There are some boats coming up the river now!" interrupted Andy.

"Great! It's the marine construction gang!" Duffy cheered. "Now we'll really get going. They're here!" he shouted to the other workmen. "They're here!"

Everyone stopped working and ran to the shore of the river. They waved and hollered at them. Andy was so excited he shouted too. Derrick boats, scows and barges loaded with machines and equipment filed by and whistled.

"The floating construction equipment builds the foundations of the bridge right in the river. We build on land and water at the same time," said Duffy.

"And we thought it was just talk about building a bridge." Andy, so excited a moment before, was suddenly sad. "You know, Mr. Duffy," he confided, "my Grandpa owns Binkley's Faithful Ferry up the river."

Duffy looked at him sharply. "He does?" He rubbed his jaw thoughtfully. "That's too bad. What will your Grandpa do when the ferry stops running?"

"I don't know." Andy shrugged.

On the way back, Andy thought about the new bridge and Grandpa's old ferry. He could hardly wait to tell the exciting news to his family, but he would not say anything to Grandpa just yet. He hurried back to Binkley's Landing. On the ferry, he busied himself with the motor. Then he got out a cloth and polished the ship's bell. Grandpa Binkley could tell Andy was flustered about something.

"Where were you, Andy?"

"Oh, just down the river a ways."

"What did you do there?"

"Oh — not much." Andy looked down at his sneakers.

"You were gone a mighty long time, doing not much," grumbled Grandpa.

Andy shifted uneasily from one foot to the other. Suddenly, he looked directly at Grandpa. "Gramp," he blurted out. "Gramp, they *are* beginning to build a new bridge."

Grandpa seemed to stoop over. "I know," he said in a very low voice, as he turned sadly away.

Andy got through the rest of the day somehow. He left a little before the others and ran up the hill without waiting for the rest of the family. He went directly to his Uncle Phil's gas station. Uncle Phil was filling a customer's car with gas.

"Hi, Uncle Phil!"

"Hi, Andy! Make yourself useful," invited Uncle Phil. He tossed Andy the air hose. Andy put air in the tires while Uncle Phil checked the oil and water. The lady in the car paid for the gas and drove off.

"What's on your mind, Andy?"

"They're starting work on the new bridge," began Andy. "I went down there today."

"That's good news," replied Uncle Phil, "it's about time."

Andy frowned. "Do you know what will happen to Grandpa's ferry?" He followed his uncle into the gas station.

Before he answered, Uncle Phil rang up the money in the cash register and sat down. "Andy, a new bridge with roads leading to and from it will help a great many people. There's not enough work for everyone here now, and the young folks keep leaving Springvale to get jobs in other cities."

"How would a new bridge and road help?" asked Andy.

"When transportation is better and easier, and both sides of the river are linked together, there will be a boom in the development of both the farmland and timberland. Industries, manufactured products and farm products will be nearer their markets as well as their source of supply and raw materials. Perhaps some factories will take advantage of the waterpower in the Massapee River and come here. Just think of all the people who will have jobs then! And with more people working here, the local stores and businesses will thrive. Also, people on vacation will be encouraged to come to this part of the country and use our fine roads and bridge."

Andy listened carefully. He had never thought of all those things. "So that's the way

our country grows!" he remarked. "But with all the new jobs, what about Grandpa? He's been a ferryman all his life."

"I know," Uncle Phil shook his head, "and Grandpa won't want to do anything that will take him away from his beloved river."

As the days and weeks went by, Andy thought a great deal about the new bridge. He also worried about Grandpa Binkley and his ferry. Instead of the State buying a new ferry, a new bridge was bought and Grandpa was left out.

"I'll have to think of something to help Grandpa," Andy said to himself, "for neither Grandpa nor anyone else is."

He wondered how the construction was coming on and how much was finished on the bridge but he didn't want Grandpa to know he was so interested. One day after school, he stuffed an apple and a bar of chocolate into his pocket. Instead of going by boat, he followed the Indian trail along the river bank to the bridge site. The Indian trail was only a clearing which occasionally got lost in a tangle of low spreading branches — or else it disappeared altogether into the water when craggy rocks blocked the path and fell down sharply into the river. Then Andy took off his shoes and socks and waded in the cool, shallow water. The tiny minnows, frightened, scurried away under the ripples. Up again, Andy climbed on the soft moss and sweet-smelling

pine needles. When he got past the bend of the river he saw work going on all over. The trees had been cleared away right down to the river.

A workman came over. "Looking for someone, Buddy?"

"Is Mr. Duffy here?"

"There he is, near the shack."

At that moment, Duffy saw Andy. "Hi, Andy! Have you come to inspect the job?"

Andy grinned. "Gee, there's a lot going on! I don't know how anybody knows what he's doing. It all looks so mixed up and busy."

Duffy laughed. "Come, let's look around. Every bit of construction is carefully planned. Each man has his job to do. They work in crews. Now here, we're standing where the approach to the bridge will be."

Andy watched the huge machines at work. A power shovel swung its long arm to pick up the blasted chunks of rock and drop them into waiting trucks. "It must be fun to operate that crane!" Andy looked longingly at the young man in the power shovel cab.

The young man waved at him. "Wanna come up here?"

Andy didn't need to be asked twice. Duffy helped him climb up and squeeze next to the driver. Andy saw it took a lot of practice to work the long boom to pick up the rocks and dump them into the truck and not on someone's head!

Further inland, Andy saw the highway taking shape. A wide path had been cleared through forest, hills and rocky mountains. Big pan-scrapers were moving more dirt in an hour than a crew of men could have done in a day years

ago. Heavy rollers weighing many tons tamped down the earth, packing it down hard. A grader leveled and curved the sides of the road.

Finally, a large strip was ready for surfacing. As each part was done, the machines moved off to work on a new section of the road, with teamwork all along the line.

After watching a while, Duffy suggested they go down to the loading and unloading dock along the river. Barges and tugs carried supplies to the men working in the river and across on the other side. The storage area nearby contained piles of all kinds of equipment, various machines and tools. There was even a machine shop to take care of repairs and a concrete-mixing plant.

"In the river," said Duffy, "you have the real beginnings of the bridge itself."

"What's that enormous thing out there?" asked Andy, pointing.

"That's a caisson. It's a steel box with no top or bottom. It was built on land and floated out into the water. The men will sink it down to the river bottom. When the water is pumped out of it the men, called sandhogs, will go down inside to dig up the river bed until they come to bedrock for the foundation of the bridge to rest on. The caisson itself will be sunk deeper and deeper, then left in and filled with concrete. In that way it becomes the foundation. This bridge will have two foundation piers — one either side of the river. A tower will be built on each one, up out of the water and high in the air. From these two towers the bridge roadway is hung or suspended."

"I suppose that gives it its name of 'Suspension Bridge,'" said Andy.

Duffy laughed. "You'll become an engineer yourself by the time the bridge is finished."

It was time for Andy to go back. He sprinted down the Indian trail, his ears ringing with the

rut-dut-dut of the tremendous machines, his
head full of the wonderful road and the remark-
able bridge. However, as he approached Binkley's Faithful Ferry softly chugging across the
river in its unhurried way, he felt perhaps it was
wrong to be so happy about a bridge that would
stop the little ferry from running and push
Grandpa right off the river.

Spring turned into summer. School was over.
The corn grew tall on the hillside. The fruit
hung heavy in the trees. The katydids kept up
their ceaseless rasping to remind everyone how
hot it was. The city people flocked to the country. Some stayed around Springvale. Many
others crossed the Massapee River on Binkley's

Faithful Ferry and went on their way. The ferry was so busy the cars sometimes queued up for miles bumper to bumper, on each side of the river — waiting, complaining, waiting. Still others traveled many miles out of their way to avoid being held up by "Binkley's Bottleneck." Tempers grew short while cars overheated.

Andy was down at the river all day. He helped Grandpa Binkley run the ferry. At times he swam and fished with the boys and girls or went on a picnic. But he could not keep away from the new bridge. The Indian trail in the woods along the Massapee River became a well-worn path. Every few days, early in the morning before it got too hot, Andy tramped down the Indian trail to the bridge. He watched it grow and take form. The caissons, weighted with concrete, were sunk in place. Duffy explained how the men who worked in them had to go down

through several chambers or rooms with sealed doors so they could become gradually accustomed to the changes in air pressure. The deeper the sandhogs worked, the less time they were permitted to remain on the bottom, the air pressure was so great. If such care were not taken they would get dreadfully ill.

Other sections of the highway were started on both sides of the river. After the roadway was rolled smooth and level to make a solid base, the huge roadlayer machine mixed tons of concrete. It was dumped on the roadbed from a large bucket on a long boom. Mats of steel strips were laid over this and again concrete was poured over. Then the "finishers" moved behind the roadlayer, spreading and smoothing the concrete to make it fine and hard.

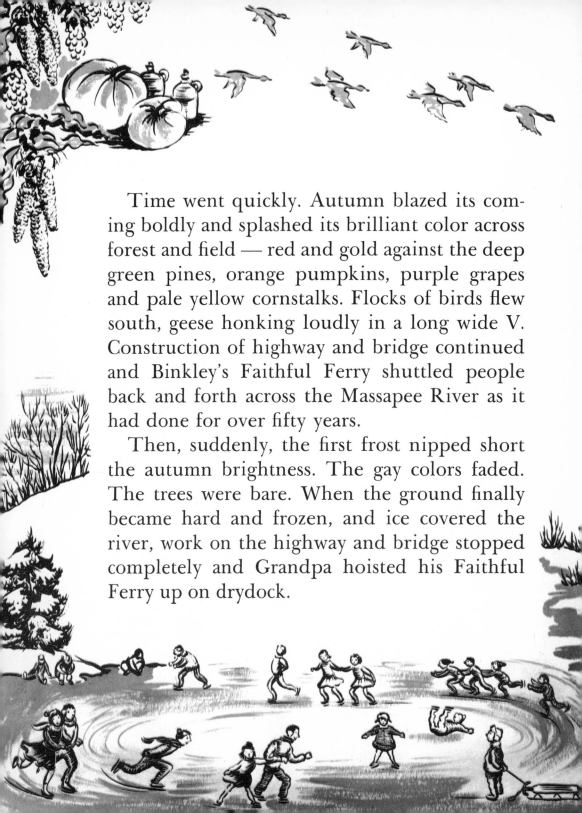

Time went quickly. Autumn blazed its coming boldly and splashed its brilliant color across forest and field — red and gold against the deep green pines, orange pumpkins, purple grapes and pale yellow cornstalks. Flocks of birds flew south, geese honking loudly in a long wide V. Construction of highway and bridge continued and Binkley's Faithful Ferry shuttled people back and forth across the Massapee River as it had done for over fifty years.

Then, suddenly, the first frost nipped short the autumn brightness. The gay colors faded. The trees were bare. When the ground finally became hard and frozen, and ice covered the river, work on the highway and bridge stopped completely and Grandpa hoisted his Faithful Ferry up on drydock.

In former years, when winter closed in around Springvale the village slowed down to a leisurely pace. But this winter was different. In another year the highway and bridge would be completed and ready for public use. This started a boom of business activity.

At the supper table one night Andy started with, "A paper manufacturing company is going to build a factory and mill on the shores of the Massapee. There will be hundreds of wonderful jobs." He hoped to raise a spark of interest in Grandpa but succeeded only in arousing the interest of the family. Grandpa kept his eyes on his soup.

"They're building hundreds of new homes to take care of all the people coming to Springvale to work," said Father Binkley.

"I hear a chain of super markets opened a store on Main Street," added Mother, "and our butcher says he won't be outdone; he and Mr. Dodds the grocer and the vegetable man next door are pooling all their savings to open a modern, self-service, *super-duper* super market — as he calls it."

Paul perked up. "I'd like to work in the new

dairy and ice-cream plant that's coming to Appleby Hills."

"You're not old enough," said Ellie. "Besides, do you think they'd let you eat ice cream all day?"

Grandpa Binkley did not join in the family's enthusiasm. He finished his supper and went to his room. Andy's heart sank.

As Springvale grew, the village departments expanded too; the fire and police departments, public works and schools. Money came rolling in from the taxes on new homes and businesses. The School Board voted on a brand new school to take care of all the additional children.

Even Uncle Phil and Andy's father got together on a large new gas and service station. It would be built where the cut-in to Springvale branched off the new highway, not far from the entrance to the bridge.

The only man in all Springvale who didn't make any new plans — who didn't even seem to be aware of all the feverish activity around, who never spoke at all about the changes taking place, or about the new bridge, or about his own ferry — was Grandpa Binkley.

He puttered around his Faithful Ferry. He caulked the seams as he always did every year, gave it a fresh coat of paint, replaced the worn cable with new, fixed little odds and ends. When Andy dropped over to give him a hand, as he did very often, Andy still talked of new jobs. He hoped that Grandpa might like one of them.

"I see Mr. Gates has three more men helping him at his lumber yard," he said. And then, "Dad says he wishes he were twins so he could be at the boat yard and up at the new service station at the same time."

When Grandpa bothered to answer, he grumbled, "I'm a riverman. They promised me a ferry, not a bridge. There's no place for me with a bridge around."

But Andy was sure there *must* be a place for Grandpa Binkley! Some place near his river.

By the time winter was over and a fresh new spring had come, building sprouted up all over. Construction was resumed on the new highway and bridge. As soon as the ice broke up in the Massapee River, Grandpa Binkley rolled his ferry down into the water and had it running again, as busy as ever.

Every chance Andy got, he ran up to the bridge to see what was doing. The anchorages

were bolstered with steel and tons of concrete. They had to be strong enough to hold the ends of the bridge cables and to withstand the tremendous pull of the bridge's whole weight. The two foundation piers were now secure on the river bed. The superstructure, or top part of the bridge, was begun.

Before long, two steel towers rose on the foundations above the water. The sections were made far away in the steel shops and shipped to the bridge site. Tall derricks lifted each piece to the place where it was riveted to another.

The next step, after the towers were up, was to "spin" the suspension cables that would carry the weight of the bridge. Two temporary footbridges or "catwalks" were set up as working platforms by men called "riggers." These riggers

had to be as sure-footed as acrobats to work so high up! The catwalks stretched from one anchorage to the top of one tower, curved gracefully across the river to the top of the opposite tower, and sloped downward to the other anchorage. From these catwalks, the men "spun" the wires back and forth with a special machine. After thousands of wires were strung across, they were squeezed together and clamped with wire to make a fat, round cable. Steel suspender ropes were hung down from those cables to hold up the floor of the bridge.

However, as the summer passed and autumn came once more, there were so many problems, that the bridge could not be completed by winter. It was plain another winter would come and go and it was hoped the bridge would be ready by the following summer. Andy was glad, for the longer it took for the bridge to be finished the longer Binkley's Faithful Ferry would continue to run.

The twinkle came back for a while to Grandpa's eyes as he quietly said, "I guess folks still need Binkley's Faithful Ferry!"

But winter came and went. In spring, construction started once more and Binkley's Faithful Ferry ran again. In a few weeks, with work progressing smoothly, the announcement was made that the Massapee River Bridge would be open by the beginning of July.

The beginning of July! Binkley's Faithful Ferry would stop running the beginning of July, thought Andy, and what was Grandpa going to do? He spoke to Uncle Phil and his father who now spent almost all of their time up at the new gas station rushing to have it ready.

"We've asked Grandpa to come in with us," said Andy's father.

"Will he?"

"No. He said he is a riverman. He wants to work where he can see the boats going up and down the river. But a man has got to keep up with the times." He threw up his hands in despair, "Or he's left behind."

Keep up with the times. That's what Grandpa always said too — and did, thought Andy. Through all the years Grandpa had improved and enlarged his ferry. Even now, he expected a larger and faster ferry would take care of all the traffic.

"Ah!" sighed Andy one day. "If only Grandpa would *look* at the beautiful new bridge — the way it swings across the river and the highway con-

tinues right over the bridge. No waiting in line
— just stop for a second to pay the toll, and —"
Suddenly Andy stopped. *The toll.* Someone
would have to be in the toll booth to collect the
tolls! Like a flash the idea struck him. Why
couldn't Grandpa be the tollkeeper? He would
then still be working close to his beloved river.
But how could it be carried out? The Mayor of
Springvale was the one to see! Andy knew Mayor
Scott. When he wasn't busy being Mayor, he was
at his feed and grain store.

Andy dashed to the Scott Feed and Grain
Store and asked for Mayor Scott.

"Do you want to buy some grain?" asked a
salesman.

"No, I want to see Mayor Scott," replied
Andy. "It's personal," he added.

The salesman glared at him. "He isn't **here**
now, he's at his Mayor's office."

Andy thanked him and went to the village hall
in the square. He had never been inside the village hall before although he had passed by the
building many times. Men were blasting the
stone outside, cleaning it up for "Opening of
the Bridge Day." Andy entered a bare hall with

closed doors on all sides and nobody around. Just as he was wondering which door to knock upon, one of them swung open. It was an elevator.

"What can I do for you, young man?" asked the elevator man.

"I want to see Mayor Scott."

"Go in the first doorway on your left."

Andy entered a room with several people working at desks.

"What can I do for you?" asked a young lady.

"I want to see Mayor Scott."

"Have you an appointment?"

"No, ma'am."

"Just one moment, please." She gave Andy a nice smile. She made a telephone call. Then she said, "The Mayor will see you in a little while. You can sit down over there." She indicated a bench.

Andy sat and waited. He waited so long he was sure the young lady and the Mayor had forgotten all about him. He was sorry he had come. He would have slipped out of the door but for the thought of passing the young lady. At long last, the young lady said, "Go up to the second floor, turn right, and go in the second door."

Mayor Scott looked so different behind a great big desk piled with papers and framed photographs and a ship model, a brass lamp, three inkstands, a couple of ash trays full of ashes, and an assortment of what looked like toys — bears, elephants and donkeys.

"Hello, Andy!" Mayor Scott called out cheerfully. "How's Binkley's Faithful Ferry?"

"That's what I've come to see you about" — and Andy blurted out the whole story.

Mayor Scott listened, nodding his head several times, while he played with a glass paperweight. Andy was afraid he would drop it. "Good idea! I should have thought of it myself!" he said when Andy had finished. "They *will* need a toll-keeper — and Captain Binkley is the perfect man for the job. But will your grandpa agree?" When Andy looked unhappy for a moment,

Mayor Scott grinned and raised his eyebrows. "Maybe we'd better keep it a secret between you and me and then surprise him on Dedication Day."

"Yes, sir." Andy beamed. "Then Grandpa can't say no! Oh, thank you, Mayor, I knew you would be able to do it!" Andy fairly danced with joy as he scooted out of the village hall and skipped home.

The last few weeks before Dedication Day were hectic. The links of the new highway were connected and the gently curving, gently rising ribbon of road swept up to the new bridge, crossed the Massapee River and led gently down the other side, through the hills and away to distant cities. The workmen rushed with the finishing touches. The sides of the highway were landscaped and planted with grass and shrubs. Guardrails of steel cables painted white were put up at the necessary places, the route numbers and directional signs were installed and, lastly, the white line was painted down the center of the new pavement.

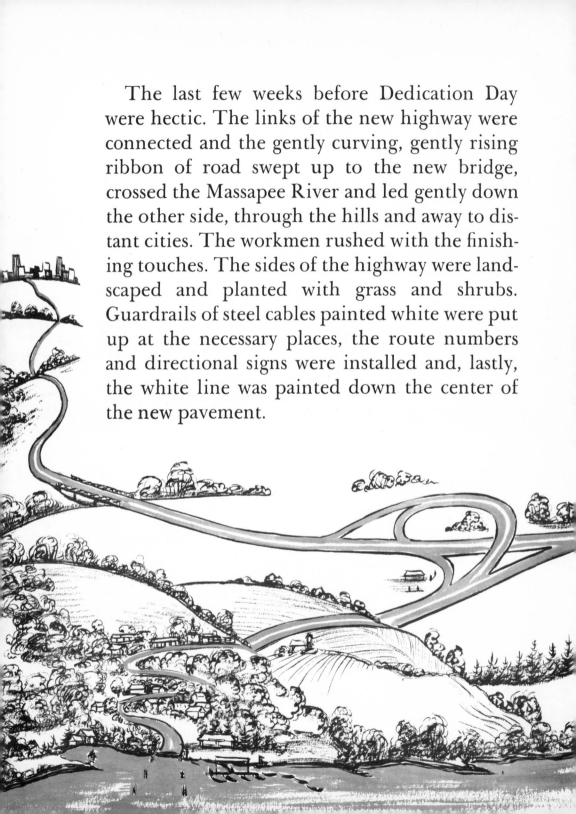

On the bridge the four-lane roadway and sidewalk were finished, the electric lights and telephone system were rigged up, and an American flag was flown from the highest point.

At last the great day arrived. The shops were closed and hung with banners which read, OPENING OF THE MASSAPEE RIVER BRIDGE. Colored streamers framed the windows. American flags waved from every house. It was a great day for all the people of the whole countryside. They had been preparing for the opening celebration for weeks.

Andy was so excited he changed his tie three times. Then he clamored loudly, "Who took my red belt?" running all over the house looking for it — and all the time he was wearing it! His brother Paul was going to march with the Boy Scouts in the Grand Parade, and his sister Ellie still couldn't make up her mind whether to march with the Girl Scouts or sit with the rest of the family in the grandstand. She finally decided to march in the parade.

Grandpa Binkley had been invited to ride in one of the official automobiles because he was the oldest resident of Springvale. Mother Binkley wanted him to wear his uniform from the Spanish-American War of 1898 — he looked so important and handsome in it. But Grandpa boomed "*No*, I won't!" And that was that. "Furthermore," he declared, "I'm not going to ride in any parade. What's all this fuss about a new bridge?"

"Do you think he means that?" Mother whispered anxiously to Father. "It would be *so* embarrassing if he didn't show up!"

"Ssh, let's not say anything more to him." Father was so nervous he dropped his cuff link

and had to dive under the bureau to reach it.

"Grandpa *must* ride in the parade!" Andy was frantic. "Mom, Dad — there's going to be a *surprise* and Grandpa is *in* it!"

"What surprise?" his mother started to ask.

"Ssh, everything's going to be all right — I hope. Now let's get dressed." Father dropped the other cuff link.

Finally the Binkleys were ready. They piled into their car, Grandpa too, in his best Sunday suit but with his old captain's cap defiantly topping his white head. Friends and neighbors crowded the road all the way into the village. They shouted excitedly, "Hi there!" or "Isn't the weather just perfect?" or "See you at the bridge!" Little children waved flags or tooted toy horns.

Those in the Grand Parade were to assemble in the square in front of the village hall. Paul, Ellie and Grandpa were dropped off there while Mother, Father and Andy went on to the grandstand built for the dedication ceremony on the bridge plaza.

"See you at the bridge!" Andy waved his hand to Grandpa. Grandpa didn't answer. He didn't even smile. Andy had a funny feeling as they drove away. He turned around and looked back; he saw Grandpa mingle with the crowd, then he was out of sight.

The Grand Parade was to start at the village hall, go along the new road to the new highway to the wide plaza of the bridge. Cars from all over lined the shoulders of the roads, with chil-

dren comfortably perched on the tops. Motorcycle policemen scooted up and down keeping
the center of the road cleared for moving ve-
hicles. The Binkleys found seats in the grandstand. They had come none too soon, the
benches filled up so quickly.

Andy couldn't sit still. He ran down to the
road at least ten times to see if the parade was
coming. "That won't make the parade come any
faster," observed Mother. "Do sit still. You're
annoying all the people."

"It won't be long now," said Father, several
times.

"Here it comes! Here it comes!" Andy jigged
up and down.

With a scream of sirens, two motorcycle policemen cleared the road. Dozens of little children hastily squatted along the edge. A squad of motorcycle policemen smartly criss-crossed each other up the highway, ending in a single formation. Then they formed doubles, then they came riding four abreast, then eight. Everyone applauded.

"Can you hear the band?" asked Andy of everyone. "Here's the band! Here it comes!"

Boom! Boom! Ta-ta-room-boom-boom! The high school band, all blue and gold, boomed along, led by a pretty, strutting, golden-haired majorette. How she twirled her baton, threw it up high, and caught it! Then came the massed colors — dozens of color bearers carrying large American flags. Everyone stood up and saluted. Andy couldn't see a thing. He climbed on top of the bench. Ah, that was better.

Then came the cars, draped in red, white and blue. There was the Mayor. Hurrah for Mayor Scott! The Governor of the State was with him, and another man. They all wore tall silk hats. They nodded and smiled and waved.

Where was Grandpa? Well, maybe he would be in the next car.

Senator Miller and Judge Mackay and Mr. Somebody-or-other were in the next car, smiling and tipping their hats, but no Grandpa.

And the next car passed and the next car — and still no sign of Grandpa. Mother and Father exchanged nervous glances. Andy asked, "Where's Grandpa?" The important people who arrived in the cars now took their seats on the platform. Mayor Scott caught Andy's eye and shrugged with outspread hands. They plainly said, "Where's Grandpa?"

The marines were coming now, led by a

snappy marine band. Andy slipped unnoticed from his seat. He climbed down behind the grandstand and scrambled down the hill, along the concrete and steel anchorage of the bridge, down to the river bank. He was soon on his old Indian path. He raced wildly back toward Binkley's Landing. He did not care that his good jacket was torn by thorns and sharp branches, that his legs were bruised scraping across the rocks. He splashed through the shallow water where the path fell away and didn't stop to take off his socks or shoes.

He just had to find Grandpa, and he thought he knew where he would be.

Binkley's Landing looked deserted. The empty boats rocked gently with the breeze, the river slapped at the vacant docks and piers. Andy ran onto the ferry. "Grandpa! Grandpa!" he called, breathless and half sobbing. "Grandpa!"

"Andy, what are you doing here?" Grandpa came out of the cabin. He looked so old and drooping.

"Oh, Grandpa, come back!" cried Andy. "They're all waiting for you."

"No, son, they don't need me any more —

not me nor my ferry. When I was up there in the square getting ready for the parade, I just couldn't go through with it, so I came down here."

"Grandpa, you've been in Springvale longer than anybody else. It's grown. The whole country has grown. The new bridge is progress. You said so yourself. You said you've always kept up with the times. Don't let us down!"

Grandpa watched Andy as he pleaded with him. It was as if he were seeing him clearly for the first time in a very long long time. Suddenly, he smiled and gave Andy a quick hug. "Binkley keeps up with progress — let's go! Where are they up to now?"

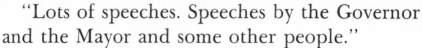

"Lots of speeches. Speeches by the Governor and the Mayor and some other people."

"What's the quickest way to get there?" asked Grandpa. They both looked at the ferry and burst out laughing. "Why not?"

"Grandpa, can the ferry go down the river without a cable, on its own power?"

"Sure, it has a rudder. And we won't need the cable any more anyhow." Grandpa snapped the cable in two and let it slip into the water. He nosed the ferry around towards the bridge. "Ho ho! What a wonderful idea! The two Binkleys go to the opening of the Massapee River Bridge on Binkley's Faithful Ferry." The twinkle had come back to Grandpa's eyes.

It didn't take long for the empty ferry to chug downstream with the current. As they approached the bridge, Grandpa rang the ship's bell loud and long.

Mayor Scott was in the middle of a speech. He recognized the bell of Binkley's Faithful Ferry, as did everyone else from the surrounding countryside. "Ladies and gentlemen," the Mayor announced, "I believe someone we've been waiting for has arrived!"

Grandpa and Andy tied up the ferry to a rock under the bridge. "This is a fine way to dock a ferry!" laughed Grandpa as they both waded into the water to shore. Grandpa looked up; a great many people were watching them, smiling, calling and waving merrily. "What's all this — ?"

Andy took him firmly by the hand. There was no turning back now. They climbed up the embankment, over the top railing to the bridge plaza. Andy prodded Grandpa on to the grandstand.

Everyone clapped and shouted and the band played "For He's a Jolly Good Fellow." Mayor Scott looked at Grandpa's wet trousers. "Looks like our new tollkeeper was in such a hurry to get here, he swam." There was loud laughter.

Mayor Scott led Grandpa to the Governor, who stood next to a golden ribbon stretched across the opening of the bridge. The Governor had a huge shining scissors in his hand.

"— and now I officially open this history-making span, the Massapee River Bridge —" he snipped the golden ribbon in two — "and it is my pleasure to invite all of you and the whole traveling public to use this bridge to open up a happy and prosperous future." Applause. "This great bridge has cost millions of dollars, yet it will pay for itself in tolls."

He paused and smiled. "Now it is my great pleasure to install the first tollkeeper of the Massapee River Bridge — a man who has greeted

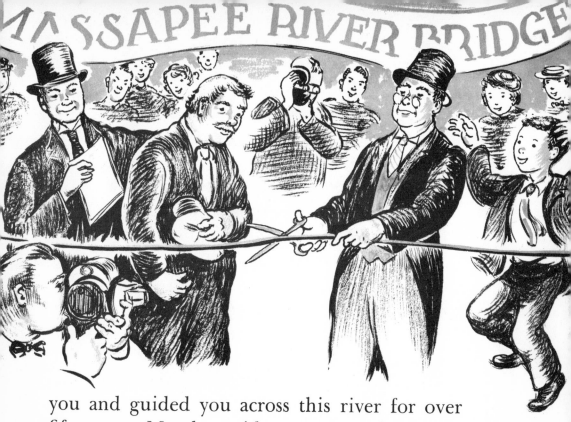

you and guided you across this river for over
fifty years. May he guide you across for many,
many more years. CAPTAIN EVERETT BINKLEY!"

Everyone clapped and shouted.

"Hooray for Grandpa!" whooped Andy. He
was so excited, he thought he'd burst. "I knew
it before. It was a secret between Mayor Scott
and me," he whispered hoarsely to his mother
and father.

"Now everyone may go across the Massapee
River Bridge — this is your big chance without
paying a toll!" declared Mayor Scott.

Grandpa Binkley and Andy walked together to the new toll booth. They went inside and looked out of the large picture window. "This is a mighty fine bridge," said Grandpa, all choked up. "Look at the wonderful view of the river you can get from up here. I can see the boats coming miles up and down the river. This *is* progress, Andy."

"Grandpa," said Andy, "I used to think that when I grew up I would run a ferry like you did. Now I think I'm going to a be a bridge engineer and build bridges."

Grandpa chuckled, "Whatever you do, Andy, keep up with the times!"